PIPPI LONGSTOCKING'S
After-Christmas Party

ASTRID LINDGREN

Translated from the Swedish by Stephen Keeler

Illustrated by Michael Chesworth

PUFFIN BOOKS

TRANSLATOR'S NOTE

Christmastime in Sweden is celebrated with a number of unique traditions. One typically Swedish Christmas tradition is that of stripping or "plundering" the tree before it is taken down. And that's why Pippi's party is an after-Christmas party.

PUFFIN BOOKS

Published by the Penguin Group
Penguin Putnam Inc., 375 Hudson Street, New York, New York 10014, U.S.A.
Penguin Books Ltd, 27 Wrights Lane, London W8 5TZ, England
Penguin Books Australia Ltd, Ringwood, Victoria, Australia
Penguin Books Canada Ltd, 10 Alcorn Avenue, Toronto, Ontario, Canada M4V 3B2
Penguin Books (N.Z.) Ltd, 182-190 Wairau Road, Auckland 10, New Zealand

Penguin Books Ltd, Registered Offices: Harmondsworth, Middlesex, England

First published in Sweden by Raben and Sjogren, 1950
English translation first published in Great Britain by Penguin Books Ltd., 1995
Hardcover edition with illustrations by Michael Chesworth first published in the United States of America by Viking,
a division of Penguin Books USA Inc., 1996
Published by Puffin Books, a member of Penguin Putnam Books for Young Readers, 1998

1 3 5 7 9 10 8 6 4 2

THE LIBRARY OF CONGRESS HAS CATALOGED THE VIKING EDITION AS FOLLOWS:
Lindgren, Astrid.
[Pippi har julgransplundring. English]
Pippi's after-Christmas party / by Astrid Lindgren;
illustrated by Michael Chesworth; translated by Stephen Keeler. p. cm.
Summary: Pippi Longstocking's after-Christmas party includes such activities as
undecorating the Christmas tree, opening presents, and sledding.
ISBN 0-670-86790-X
[1. Christmas—Fiction.] I. Chesworth, Michael, ill. II. Keeler, Stephen. III. Title.
PZ7.L6585Pm 1996 [E]—dc20 96-16308 CIP AC
Puffin Books ISBN 0-14-056425-X

Printed in the United States of America

To my family.
— M. C.

My thanks to Birgitta Dalin
for her invaluable assistance,
and to Astrid Lindgren
for her encouragement.   — S. K.

ne day during the Christmas holidays something quite remarkable happened in the little town of Villekulla. A big notice was pinned to the door of the little town hall which stood in the market square. On the notice was written:

PIPPI LONGSTOCKING
is HAVING AN
AFTER-CHRISTMAS
PARTY TONIGHT.
AT VILLA VILLEKULLA
ALL CHILDREN IN TOWN
ARE WELCOME.
BRING WARM CLOTHES

Pippi hadn't actually written the notice herself, you understand. She would never have been able to spell "Christmas" properly. Tommy had helped her.

All day long, children came and stood in front of the town hall and studied the notice. When they had read it they each gave out a shrill cry of joy and ran home as fast as their legs would carry them to tell their parents about the invitation and make them promise to let them go.

Tommy and Annika had known for a long time that Pippi was planning to have an after-Christmas party, but they were just as impatient as everyone else. They stayed at home and waited and waited for the evening to come. Normally, they would have been at Pippi's house all day, but she had already told them that she wanted to be alone so she could get everything ready for the party.

A lot of snow had fallen during the Christmas holidays, but on the night of the party, as all the children set off for Villa Villekulla, the starry sky was clear and still; the winter's night was crisp and chill.

Tommy and Annika led the way. But as Tommy was opening the garden gate to Villa Villekulla he suddenly stopped and gave a little cry of despair. What was this? There was no light shining in Pippi's window, not even the tiniest glimmer. The cottage stood silent among the snow-laden trees, and everything seemed completely lifeless.

The children began to feel uneasy. "Perhaps we've come on the wrong night," said one little boy, "and Pippi's after-Christmas party isn't until tomorrow."

Oh, how disappointing! Especially since they'd been looking forward to it so much.

Tommy jumped onto the veranda and tried the door. It was locked! One little girl was so unhappy she began to cry.

Well, there was nothing to do but go back home. They turned to go, an unusually gloomy little group of children trying not to show how sad they were.

And then, suddenly, Pippi's little monkey, Mr. Nilsson, leapt into view wearing a thick suit which Pippi had made for him to keep out the winter cold.

Mr. Nilsson jumped up onto Tommy's shoulder and handed him a slip of paper. It said, in great big letters,

FOLLO THE TRALE AND EET IT UP.

The spelling was a bit strange, but Tommy understood that it meant "Follow the trail and eat it up!" But what trail? And what did it mean by "eat it up"? You can't very well eat up a trail, can you?

"Look!" shrieked Tommy, suddenly. "There! Look, in the snow!"

And sure enough, there on the white snow lay a wandering red trail, a trail of red toffee candies that disappeared behind the back of Villa Villekulla. A minute later the children had eaten up the trail right around to the back of the house, and there—yes—there behind the house they almost choked on their toffee in amazement.

"A Christmas tree," whispered Annika. "Oh, a beautiful Christmas tree!"

There were, in fact, many trees in Pippi's garden, but right behind the house there stood a Christmas tree, a beautiful, tall, dark green Christmas tree. Candlelight shone brightly from it, not from the usual tiny little Christmas-tree candles but from great big bright candles that lit up the whole garden.

And there weren't only candles on the tree, either. There were great big gingerbread men and huge baskets made of tin foil and enormous twists of toffee and, of course, lovely Christmas crackers that you pull at each end. And the tree was hung with strands of tiny little flags. But, most curious of all, hanging from all the branches there were dozens of presents!

At first the children just stood in silence. But then they began to squeal with joy.

"Oh, how kind of Pippi!" they shouted.

Pippi? Oh, yes! Where was Pippi? She still wasn't any-where to be seen. But right next to the Christmas tree there was a large igloo which Pippi and Tommy and Annika had built. And now a little light shone through the igloo's tiny window, and a red head popped out of the entrance.

"Would anyone like some hot chocolate and cream cake before we dance around the tree?" shouted Pippi.

Yes, all the children wanted hot chocolate and cream cake, and one after another they crept into the igloo.

"Didn't we build a great igloo?" said Tommy, pleased with himself, as he sat down on the floor with all the others. Everyone agreed. It really was a very fine igloo indeed.

Pippi had a large pan full of piping hot chocolate on the floor in front of her, and an enormous cream cake. She was just about to start serving when she glanced through one of the windows of the igloo.

Over by the corner of the house stood a little boy. He had only just moved to the little town a couple of days before and didn't know Pippi, and therefore he *knew* that the invitation to Pippi's after-Christmas party couldn't possibly include him. He had gone

around with tears in his eyes the whole day, and when evening had come he couldn't resist following the other children, just to *look*. He didn't intend to be spotted by anyone. And now he was standing there by the corner of the house looking at the magnificent Christmas tree and the lovely igloo where all the children were talking, and suddenly he felt an awful lump in his throat. At that moment Pippi caught sight of him.

The little boy was terrified as she crept out of the igloo.

His first thought was to turn and run, but in fact, he couldn't bear to tear himself away.

"Who are you?" asked Pippi.

"I'm called Elof," said the boy, "but . . . I haven't touched anything."

And then, before he knew what he was saying, he asked, "I wondered if I could come into your igloo for a little while if I promise not to eat anything?" The question was out before he had time to stop it, because he so much wanted to go into the igloo, even for just a little while.

"Not on your life!" said Pippi.

And that was just what Elof had feared, and now the lump in his throat grew even bigger.

"Not on your life can you come into the igloo if you promise *not* to eat anything," said Pippi. "But if you promise to eat more than anyone else, well then you'd be very welcome!"

And then she led Elof into the igloo, where he sat down among all the others and stuffed himself so full of hot chocolate and cake that there was no room left for the lump in his throat, and his eyes shone as brightly as the candles which Pippi had set into the snow walls of the big igloo.

But there was someone else who wanted to come to Pippi's after-Christmas party.

Even as the children sat there and talked they heard a sad and sorry howling cry coming from outside. Pippi crept out to see who was making such a sad and sorry sound. It was a dog, a shaggy black dog, sitting in the snowdrift and looking so sad. Pippi reached out her hand to him.

"Come to Pippi and tell me all about it," she said.

And, do you know, the black dog came to Pippi and in two leaps had snuggled up onto her lap just as though he had always wanted to do exactly that. He whimpered and snuffled as though he was trying to tell her why he was so sad.

"Oh, really, is that right?" said Pippi. "You poor thing!"

"Is what right?" asked Tommy. "Can you really understand what he's saying?"

"Why shouldn't I understand when someone says something to me in perfect Swedish?" asked Pippi. "He says his name is Perk and he's completely alone without anyone to care for him and he's been wandering around in the snow for three days and is so awfully hungry and thirsty and that he would like to become my pet dog, if I want him."

"Oh, Pippi, do let him be your pet," pleaded Annika.

Pippi took Perk's head in her hands and looked him straight in the eyes.

"Of course he can be my pet," she said. And Perk jumped up and barked and wagged his tail and tried to lick Pippi's hair and face and forehead, and they rolled around together in the snow until Perk was no longer a sad black dog but a happy white dog, his fur full of snow. Pippi ran into Villa Villekulla to get a couple of large pieces of meat for Perk to eat instead of cream cake, and a large bowl of milk to drink. He was so happy. He spent the rest of the evening creeping in and out of the igloo and scampering about among the children. He even stepped in a cream cake in his excitement.

"Just think, Pippi," said Tommy, "now you've got a dog and a horse and a monkey at Villa Villekulla."

"Yes. All that's missing now is a crocodile and a couple of small rattlesnakes," said Pippi contentedly.

"Oh no, Pippi, don't get any rattlesnakes," shrieked Annika, altogether scared out of her wits. "Then I'd never dare come here again."

"You never know," said Pippi. "Perhaps one fine day a rattlesnake will come by and cry and beg for me to let him stay here and be a necklace for me."

"Oh, my goodness me," said Elof. "Pippi, what are you saying?"

"I can never say no," said Pippi. "I should have to welcome a rattlesnake, too."

"Oof!" said Annika. "Horrible!"

"Well, let's not worry about that now," said Pippi. "Now we must eat more cake."

Well now, there was yet one more person who wanted to come to Pippi's after-Christmas party. Not far from Villa Villekulla there lived a very bad-tempered old woman called Mrs. Finkvist. She didn't like children at all. There shouldn't even be any children, she thought. Every time a few children went down the street past her house she would stick her head out the window and scold them for making too much noise. And of all the children there were, Mrs. Finkvist thought Pippi Longstocking was absolutely the worst.

Now it just so happened that on the night of Pippi's after-Christmas party Mrs. Finkvist had gone out for a short evening walk past Villa Villekulla, just as all the cake had run out in the igloo and Pippi had run into the house to fetch three

more cakes she had kept aside just in case. Pippi came out through the door with a cake in each hand and one balanced on her head just as Mrs. Finkvist was passing by. You can imagine how she looked at Pippi. Mrs. Finkvist didn't like Pippi. She didn't like children. But there was something that she *did* like and that was cream cakes. She was so crazy about cream cakes that she would do anything just to get even a tiny little bit.

"Hey you, listen!" shrieked Mrs. Finkvist. "If you ask me *very* nicely I *could* come and join your after-Christmas party."

Just that morning Mrs. Finkvist had shouted "horrid child" at Pippi, but right now she had forgotten all about that. Just because of the cream cakes, you understand.

Pippi stopped dead in her tracks. She stood upright with her head in the air so that the cream cake was about to slide off. All the children had gathered by the corner of the house and were peering around it.

"My dear Mrs. Finkvist," said Pippi very politely, "this after-Christmas party is for children only. In fact, grown-ups are absolutely forbidden. And, as a matter of fact, it is not good for grown-ups to eat cream cakes and toffee. They only give you a tummy ache and make you irritable. At least that's what the doctors say," said Pippi.

"Rubbish!" cried Mrs. Finkvist.

"Oh no," said Pippi, very earnestly. "There is a doctor in America who has discovered that grown-ups should only eat boiled fish and stewed carrots. Perhaps a little fish pie on their birthdays."

"Oh, is that so?" said Mrs. Finkvist sourly. "And this doctor of yours in America, what does he say about what children should eat?"

"Candy for breakfast, ice cream for lunch, and cream cakes for supper!" said Pippi as she disappeared behind the house.

"Horrid child!" shrieked Mrs. Finkvist.

"Now it's time to try out my sledding track," said Pippi, after Mrs. Finkvist had gone.

Pippi had made a sledding track on the roof of Villa Villekulla. It was the highest and steepest sledding track the children had seen in their lives, and as slippery as could be. You could even slide down it without a sled. Of course, you had to clamber up a little ladder to get onto the roof, and that was a bit awkward, but going down was so much faster! It was such fun and all the children became so warm and so red in their cheeks and so white on their bottoms, and the Christmas tree stood there glistening so beautifully against the dark. You could see it even better from the roof. Yes, you could see even better just how many presents were hanging on its branches.

And it gave them all a little thrill when they thought about what they might possibly find inside those parcels.

"Oh, we've forgotten to dance around the Christmas tree," shouted Pippi suddenly. And all at once the children tumbled down the steep slope of the roof together, like rolling peas, and landed in the snowdrift below.

"Hey, everyone!" shouted Pippi, "come over here and let's hear some of those good old songs. 'We three kings of Orient are, one on a bicycle, two in a car...'"

"No, Pippi, that's not right at all," said Annika crankily.

"Isn't it?" asked Pippi. "Have I forgotten all those good old songs? No, of course not. I remember now: 'I saw three ships come sailing in with Rudolph the Red-Nosed Reindeer and Jingle Bells around his neck, around his neck, around his neck, Jingle Bells around his neck, fa-la-la-la-lay.' Oh it's such fun."

"Oh Pippi, how silly you are. That's not right at all," said Annika.

But dancing around the Christmas tree went well, and even though Pippi mixed up the words a bit they sang one song after another. "We Three Kings" and "I Saw Three Ships" and "Rudolph the Red-Nosed Reindeer" and "Jingle Bells." And everyone agreed that it was much more fun to dance around the Christmas tree when it was outside.

Then it was time for the very best thing of all. The presents!

All the children scrambled up the Christmas tree and took a present for themselves. If there was anyone who was a bit scared to climb so high, then Mr. Nilsson was very happy to climb up and fetch the present down.

Oh how exciting it was to open all those presents, and what great things were in them!

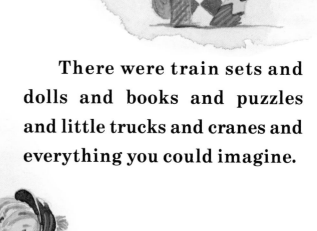

There were train sets and dolls and books and puzzles and little trucks and cranes and everything you could imagine.

Then all that remained was to strip the tree of everything that was left on it.

"It's definitely much more fun stripping the tree when you can climb up it," said Tommy as he eased himself very carefully along a branch to reach a piece of toffee.

"I think so, too," said Elof as he slithered along on his stomach to reach a gingerbread man.

At last there was not so much as a Christmas cracker left on the tree. Then Pippi climbed up and blew out the candles. It became dark in the garden of Villa Villekulla. Well, not completely dark, the snow shone so white, and the stars in the sky burned so brightly.

It was time to go home. Every child had a great pile of gingerbread men and crackers and little flags to take home.

"You all look like little Christmas trees," said Pippi. And she gave each of them a candle stub, too, so that they would look even more like little Christmas trees and so that they would be able to see their way home.

The candlelight was reflected in their eyes as though the little flames flickered from within their faces as they gathered to say good-bye to Pippi.

"Thank you very much, Pippi," said Annika. "It was really wonderful."

"Yes. It really was the very best after-Christmas party I have ever been to," said Tommy.

"I think so, too," said Elof.

Perk barked and skipped around Pippi's feet. He also thought that it had been a lovely after-Christmas party. And tonight he wouldn't have to wander about alone in the streets. Tonight he would sleep on the floor next to Mr. Nilsson's little green doll's bed.

"Good night, Pippi," said the children.

"You're not too cold now, are you?" asked Pippi.

Oh no. They were not too cold. Everyone was warm. It was a fine night. The starry sky was clear and still, the winter's night was crisp and chill.